Billy

KATE DE GOLDI
Jacqui Colley

My teacher is a magnificent creature.
She lives in an ancient house with a turret and a finial, two cats, an axolotl and a kunekune pig called Daniel.
She eats black pudding and banana cake for breakfast and cold kim chee for ~~breakfast~~ lunch.
She sings KISS ME, HONEY, HONEY on the way to school and sometimes serenades us into class.
She says work should be a pleasure and play must be even better.
My Dad says they certainly broke the mould when they made Ms Love.

Ms Love says she'll give me a Jelly Snake if I let her read my latest storybook instalment.
She says she's dying for my version of Pet and Produce Day, and could it be an item in the end-of-term show?
It is ~~the~~ time people knew the truth, I say, but it may mean TWO Jelly Snakes....

End of term ev~~d~~

School photographs:
all day Monday 20th
times.This is rather
parents and caregive

Visiting Salvation
musicians are all in
Pet and Produce day
please go and talk

be d
performances w
and music. All spe
students.

Caleb Richie Room 3   A sketch about
is like a Butterfly, Room 5. A poem performed in its
Morgan Levy, Pacific Passage.   A moving true story, tol
like, titled, Room 7 A action comedy based on a rad
Lolly Leopold, Room 8 An   Free entr)
Billy Blomveld, Room 8 An action comedy based on a rad
Ricky Blomveld, Room. Last day of the term. Free entr)
titled, The Cricket.

End-of- term show. School hall. Last day of the term. Free entr)
Starting at 10.30 am followed by a later than usual morning tea bre
(tea will be served in the hall for all parents, caregivers and
grandparents).
please join us for a very musical Final Assembly.

A BUSINESS of FERRETS

KING

The

is

The TRUTH ~~MOMENT~~
by Lolly Leopold

watch like a
think like a
focus like a l
~~fix~~ like a STA
shoot

G.G.J.C

ll I never
as there ever
Cat so clever
s magical Mr M

what colour is sadness?
what colour is Love?
what colour is liberty
what colour is ~~black~~ LAughter
what colour is Lying

Pig Parade

Vietnamese Pot-Bellied Pig

Kune KUNE pig babe
photogenic

Berkshire Pig →

LADY ROBINSON APRON
① FOLD twice
② hem everywhere
button for show

9 cm

Large white ?
Large Black

AWARD winning
Ped i gree Pigs

GloucESTER old spot →

Rime against NATURE
Not Mr Mistoffelees

Long Live The King   SWEET AND CERBERUS

PINHOLE TECHNIQUES

T.S ELIOT   OLD POSSUM'S BOOK OF PRACTICAL CATS

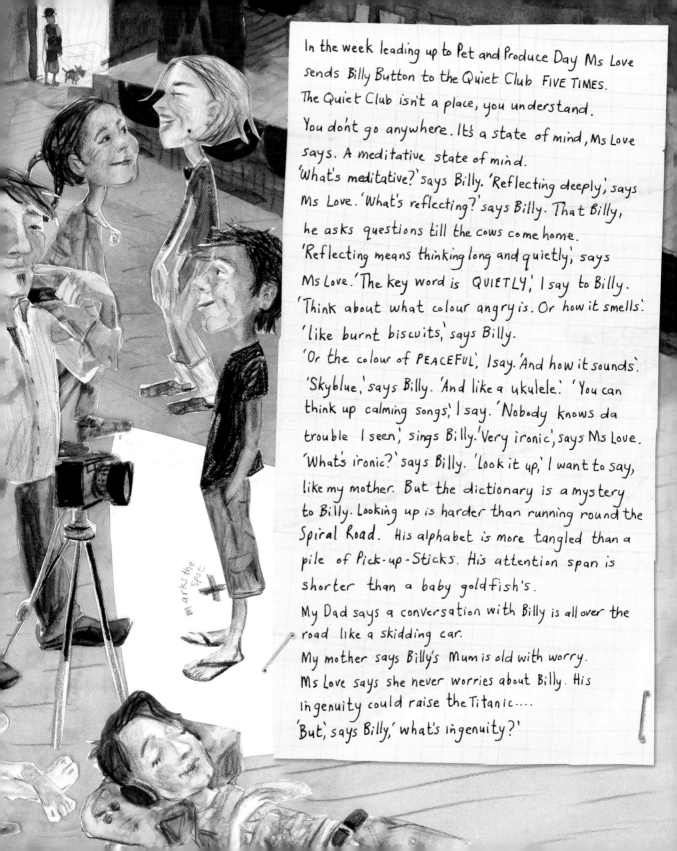

In the week leading up to Pet and Produce Day Ms Love
sends Billy Button to the Quiet Club FIVE TIMES.
The Quiet Club isn't a place, you understand.
You don't go anywhere. It's a state of mind, Ms Love
says. A meditative state of mind.
'What's meditative?' says Billy. 'Reflecting deeply,' says
Ms Love. 'What's reflecting?' says Billy. That Billy,
he asks questions till the cows come home.
'Reflecting means thinking long and quietly,' says
Ms Love. 'The key word is QUIETLY,' I say to Billy.
'Think about what colour angry is. Or how it smells.'
'Like burnt biscuits,' says Billy.
'Or the colour of PEACEFUL,' I say. 'And how it sounds.'
'Skyblue,' says Billy. 'And like a ukulele.' 'You can
think up calming songs,' I say. 'Nobody knows da
trouble I seen,' sings Billy. 'Very ironic,' says Ms Love.
'What's ironic?' says Billy. 'Look it up,' I want to say,
like my mother. But the dictionary is a mystery
to Billy. Looking up is harder than running round the
Spiral Road. His alphabet is more tangled than a
pile of Pick-up-Sticks. His attention span is
shorter than a baby goldfish's.
My Dad says a conversation with Billy is all over the
road like a skidding car.
My mother says Billy's Mum is old with worry.
Ms Love says she never worries about Billy. His
ingenuity could raise the Titanic....
'But,' says Billy, 'what's ingenuity?'

NO
flower or plant
produce to over-
hang saucer

1.
Sand mu...
a) grain
b) c...
c) de...

6.
TRADE-MARK
TOYS
PROHIBITED

Non-plant decorations
must be approved by
Sand Saucer judge
(Mrs Phyllis Wes...

...mixtures
or
...sand and soil
...mixtures

PROHIBITED!
(correct sand is available
from Mr Carrick at St
Wyn-Williams' car park after
Michaels' third Sunday
first and third service)

NO
sand to be
visible in
completed
saucer
display!

5.
...NO...

On the Monday morning before P & P Day Mrs Weston-
Wyn-Williams comes to talk about Sand Saucers.
Mrs Weston-Wyn-Williams has a long mournful face and
eyes as black as olives. She's bossier than two traffic
wardens. While she's reciting Sand Saucer rules Billy
leans over and says in a Billy whisper that ~~Mrs Weston~~
Mrs Weston-Wyn-Williams looks exactly like the
Wicked Witch of the West. Mrs Weston-Wyn-Williams
IS straight out of the Wizard of Oz, but Ms Love has no
time for loud whispering in front of visitors, so she
sends Billy to the Quiet Club.

LAY
Saucer rules
No flower or
to overhan
completed
NO more
Plagiarism
dye
wax
COMPREHENSIVE
DIAGRAM
std Saucers
Size and Shape
safe
not safe
choose your weapon!
the monkeys went to war

On Monday afternoon we construct our sand saucers.
I do my annual Memorial Library outline with linden
twigs. Adele makes secret symbols with perfectly
white pebbles. Byron has a cunning plan for a
dandelion clock face.

Billy tries a cricket game with daisies but it's a
disaster. His sand is damp and stiff and his daisies
bedraggled. When his fourth daisy falls over and a
lump of sand flicks into Freddy's lap Billy shouts
in rage, and Ms Love signals the Quiet Club again.
Ms Love says she is all for self-expression, but self-
control is a fine thing too.

My Dad says Billy's language makes him blush.
My mother says no wonder Billy's parents hardly ever
go out.

Since he's in the Quiet Club, Billy signs a swear word.

On Tuesday Dr Rolleston comes for Vegetable Exhibits.
Everyone likes Dr Rolleston, especially Billy, who has had
more stitches and injections and plaster casts than anyone
else at school.

While Dr R is demonstrating Official Radish Dimensions,
Billy leans over and whispers loudly that Dr R's nose
hair is longer and bristlier than his Gran's toothbrush.
Dr R's nasal hair is out of control, but Ms Love has
no time for unkind comments of a personal nature, so
she sends Billy to the Quiet Club for the third time.

Ladies and gentlemen

what you've all been waiting for....

But that's not all ... tell me

3098

one : glorious colour

little oil rubbed into the skin?

growing vegetablES is just like art!

everylittle bit of difference matters

Something you can't ~~touch~~ Touch or see? →

...here is the secret, this is the real truth..

two: size, magnificent size.

three: smell! you can't touch it or see
it [?] scent of your fresh Vegetable

That afternoon we fill in our entry forms. I have ~~four~~ five artwork entries. Byron and Adele enter all the cooking sections because food is their consuming passion. Alex B, Teuila and Mika devote themselves to pets. Jake will only do lego. Everyone else spreads themselves around, but Freddy gets the record: he enters Radishes, Carrots, Broad Beans, Bucket Potatoes, Shell Collection, Lego Construction, Collage, Toffee-making, Decorated Cake, Egg Art, Domestic Pet, Sand Saucer, Lamb Calling and the Lady Robinson Sewing Basket Trophy.

Freddy's list drives Billy WILD. Before we can stop him he stands on his desk and shouts that Freddy Lafu just wants to Rule the World. Which is how he ends up in the ~~Quiet~~ Quiet Club again.

My Dad says he's with Billy: Freddy's an over-achiever from way back.

Ms Love says it makes no difference if Billy mutters ~~impi~~ imprecations under his breath, hot heads require the cool reason of the Quiet Club.

'Huh,' says Billy, 'What's imprecations?'

ENTRY FORM
Pet and Produce

class teacher   Ms Love

Name   BYRON BRADSHAW

Category   EGG ART

Title   LONG LIVE THE TRUE KING

Plan   egg, fur, paint, cotton diamonds

Show costume   ELVIS car HAIR

ENTRY FORM
Pet and Produce

class Teacher   Ms Love

Name   Adele Gardner

Category   Sand Saucer

Title   A book holds a house of gold. Sand, pebbles, star

Plan   Pebbles   Secret symbol

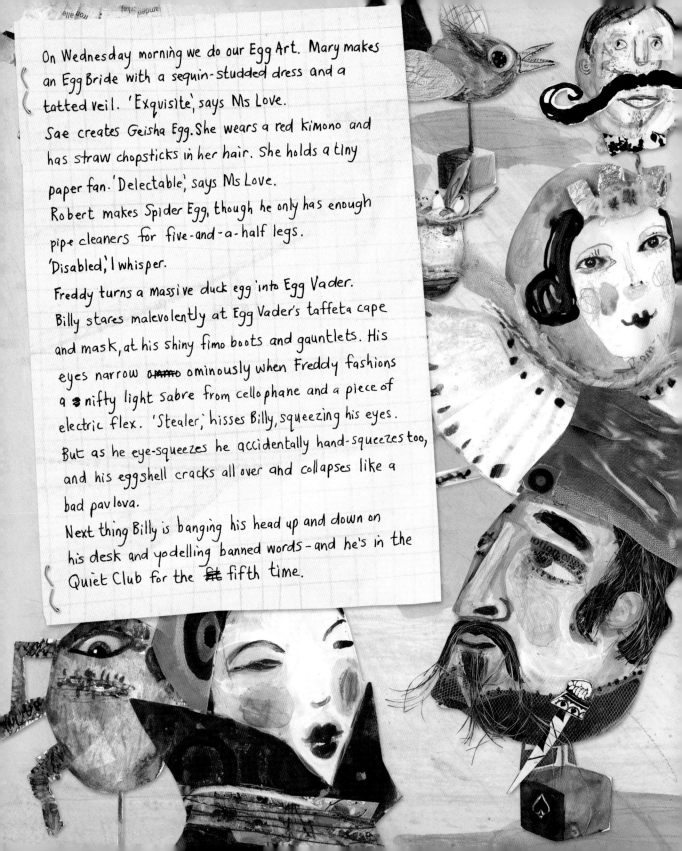

On Wednesday morning we do our Egg Art. Mary makes an Egg Bride with a sequin-studded dress and a tatted veil. 'Exquisite', says Ms Love.

Sae creates Geisha Egg. She wears a red kimono and has straw chopsticks in her hair. She holds a tiny paper fan. 'Delectable', says Ms Love.

Robert makes Spider Egg, though he only has enough pipe cleaners for five-and-a-half legs.

'Disabled,' I whisper.

Freddy turns a massive duck egg into Egg Vader. Billy stares malevolently at Egg Vader's taffeta cape and mask, at his shiny fimo boots and gauntlets. His eyes narrow ominously when Freddy fashions a nifty light sabre from cellophane and a piece of electric flex. 'Stealer,' hisses Billy, squeezing his eyes.

But as he eye-squeezes he accidentally hand-squeezes too, and his eggshell cracks all over and collapses like a bad pavlova.

Next thing Billy is banging his head up and down on his desk and yodelling banned words – and he's in the Quiet Club for the fifth time.

At lunchtime Adele and Byron and I clean the fish tank while Ms Love has a chat with Billy.

'Why do I send you to the Quiet Club, Billy?' says Ms Love.

'To help me think,' says Billy gloomily.

'Yes,' says Ms Love. 'To calm down. Smell the roses. Think.'

'I KNOW what I think,' says Billy.

'You do?' says Ms Love.

'Pet and Produce Day is like prison!' 'With no escape.'

Ms Love sighs. But next minute she's pulling Billy to his feet. 'C'mon,' she says. 'One last try? You can do it. I know you can.'

Byron hums Jailhouse Rock softly as we scrub.

We go to Billy's after school but he says he's okay and could we just write his titles?

[Titles have no rules, says Ms Love. Wit and Imagination may Run Riot.]

Billy's writing runs riot, that's for sure: it's backwards, upside down and bulges like an amoeba. But his titles are laugh-out-loud. By the time we leave Billy has four new entries ready, including a cake made with three layers and a little interference from Byron.

First up on P & P Day is the Judging.

Mrs Weston-Wyn-Williams, Dr Rolleston and Lady Robinson walk up and down the rows like policemen at a crime scene, stopping and peering, nodding, taking notes.

My Dad says the Pet and Produce judges ~~make~~ take themselves more seriously than the Nobel Prize committee.

My mother says Mrs Weston-Wyn-Williams' garden-party hat is truly a fashion crime.

Ms Love says she earnestly hopes Daniel won't try and nuzzle Lady Robinson's ample thighs during The ~~Parade~~ Parade.

At 11 a.m. the judging is complete. The first thing we see is Freddy's Decorated Cake with a blue rosette. Freddy's cake has violent red icing and is smothered in Liquorice Allsorts. It's called 'Liquorice Lunacy.' Billy's cake is called 'Nights in the Quiet Club'; it has chocolate icing as black as coffee and two Lego knights perched on top. No prize, though.

At the Egg Art table Egg Vader has a rosette tucked under his cloak.

Billy's egg doesn't have a cloak. He's called 'Quiet Egg' and has woolly hair, a black tee and a pair of long shorts like Billy's. Quiet Egg's eyes are closed and he has a fat cardboard finger to his lips- but no rosette. There are no surprises at the Sand Saucer table: Freddy scores with 'Tuatara Rex'. Billy's saucer has a ring of stones around the edge and a small black stone in the middle. It's called 'Thinking in the Quiet Club', and it doesn't have a prize.

The last table is Vegetables, where Freddy's pile of shiny broad beans has another rosette. Billy has one skinny bean pod right beside Freddy's pile. It's called 'All Alone in the Quiet Club', and next to it is a white card saying, ~~Disqua~~ Undersized - Disqualified.

'Lord love a duck,' say Byron, Adele and I at exactly the same time. [It's my mother's favourite saying in a crisis.]

'But what's disqualified?' says Billy.

While everyone is at Lamb Calling, Billy
takes his entries and throws them in
the mini bin. Then he sits under the
linden tree, not looking at the world.
'What're you thinking?' I ask.
'Of dropping something on Egg Vader
and squashing him flat,' says Billy.
Billy's Mum and Dad try to talk to
him but Billy squashes his nose against
the linden trunk.
'What are you thinking now?' asks Byron.
'That escaped lambs might eat Freddy's
vegetables,' says Billy.
Philimon offers him some third-prize
Caterpillar Cake but Billy puts his head
under his knees.
'And now?' asks Adele.
'That Tuatara Rex gets trampled by the
Patrikious twins,' says Billy.
When Ms Love comes over Billy begins yelling.
'I don't ~~care~~ CARE if you put me in the
Quiet Club!'
'What are you thinking, Billy?' says Ms Love, sitting
down beside him.
'That Freddy falls off the stage at prize-giving
and breaks both his legs,' says Billy.
'I ~~sincere~~ earnestly hope not,' says Ms Love. 'But
come to prize-giving anyway. You can carry on with
your thoughts while you're there.....'

At prize-giving Billy watches Freddy and Mika and Jake and Teuila and practically everyone in Room 7 collect prizes. The judges shake hands and pat shoulders and smilingly nod. They're like a row of factory machines — shake, shake, pat, pat, nod, nod, nod. Billy claps after every prize like a wind-up toy with flat batteries. Clap. Clap. Clap.

THE

Ingenuity

AWARD

When all the presenting and patting and nodding and shaking is over, Mr de Luca stands up.

'A Pet and Produce innovation!' he booms. 'A new award! Endowed and presented by our Junior Dean, Ms Love!'

'Freddy again,' says Billy, in a Billy Whisper.

I imagine Freddy accidentally catching fire.

Ms Love hops onto the stage, her ponytail bouncing like a horse's mane. 'Some of us work well within limits,' says Ms Love, smiling at all the ~~kids~~ faces. 'But some work brilliantly outside them.'

'What's innovation?' whispers Billy. 'What's endowed?'

'This prize,' says Ms Love, 'is for someone who has brought his life into his art.' She holds up an enormous orange rosette. The glitter falls from it like snow. 'Lord love a duck,' say Byron and Adele, but I'm holding my breath.

'Freddy,' moans Billy, diving down his tee shirt.

'This prize,' says Ms Love, 'is for someone with passion and panache who has thought well.' A sick calf sound comes from under Billy's black tee shirt.

'This prize,' says Ms Love, with a smile as wide as Birdling's Flat, 'this prize is for Billy Button.'

'Me?' says Billy, popping his head out. 'Me? ME!' he yells, leaping up onto his seat.

That Billy, he star-jumps all the way up to the judges and nearly knocks over Mr de Luca's podium.

Ms Love says that's just how she likes Pet and Produce Day to end: not with a whimper, but a bang....

My Dad says, 'I expect great things from that boy,
I really do. I see that name in lights.'
My mother says, 'Fingers crossed his ~~parents~~
parents survive.'
'What's panache?' I say.

pons Varolli
hypothalamus
thalamus
hippocampus
amygdala

BRAIN

human being

BRAINPOWER
mindread
mind or me

1. Which part manages
2. What part of the brain
3. which part handles ME
4. Which part handles

360°

Interpretation

SAMPLE 1
(born fame or fence)

E 2
ound
posting

feed in

B

Project

WAYS in

feed in

State of mind

action
reaction

colour

humanbein

process

A Feed in B procEss C PROJECT Thinking

COLOUR

Tai Tapu School Room 7
Sam Van der Velde, Lolly Leopold, Byron Bradshaw, Sae Gibbs, Joseph Wojciechowski, Billy Button, Alex McDonald, Jake Zwartz,
Danielle Jellyman, Kendal Cummings, Alexandra Bickerton, Freddy Lafu, Philamon Mbeki, Bethany Griffiths, Carla Patrikious, Tueila Heffernan Tuuilalo.
Mika Malope, Tash Herini Foster, Adele Gardener, Mary Etherington, Neha Bava, Georgie Piripi, Robert Rankin, Haami Weir.
Teacher Ms Love

INVESTIGATE

are thoughts private ??

can many people change the way the

why do ~~some~~ people think di

how can I know what some

How do some thoughts change the way

BETHANY has no brains (+ JAKE)   fact! nobrainer

Read more cat poems to Laughing Stock   relaxing in OLD age. [observe behavi

arrange collected evidence. — the truth about Pet and Produce Day — [my next book]

'Billy'

Lambcalling

Jake Zwartz
Peryman's Road
RD 2
Tai Tapu

Mrs Naomi Lopdell
97 Norman's Road
Papanui
Christchurch

November

Dear Mrs Lopdell

I hope your skirt is getting better. And your pride, which Ms Love says is gravely wounded. Everyone thinks I let Daniel out, but that's A lie. I was watching Robert in the Lamb calling with his lamb Julie Johnson. Lolly says you can actually run ~~quiet~~ quite fast. Perhaps you could join Tai Tapu harriers when you feel better. I am sorry even though I didn't do anything.

Yours sincerelly
Jake   Zwartz

Tash Hirini Foster
The Vicarage
Main Road
RD 2
Tai Tapu

Lady Caroline Robinson
'Balmoral'
Robinson Creek Road
RD2
Tai Tapu

November

Dear Lady Robinson

I am very sorry and I apologise that Daniel invaded your privacy. It must have been a very sad time for you and I would like to send my sympathy and my sorrow and my apology. I hope it is a comfort to you that so many pupils at our school entered The Lady Robinson Sewing Basket Trophy.

Yours sincerely

Tash Hirini Foster

PS. You might like to know that my Daddy Long Legs, Vanessa, won a blue rosette in the Small Pets section. It is my first ever prize.

Adele Gardner	Sam van der Velde	Mi...

Adele Gardner
Old Tai Tapu Road
RD 2
Tai Tapu

Ms Naomi Lopdell
97 Norman's Road
Papanui
Christchurch

November

Dear Mrs Lopdell

Please accept my sincere apology for the inconvenience
I may have caused you on Pet and Produce Day.
I will take much greater care next time I'm on
farmyard Duty. I am very sorry that your new skirt
was torn by the barbed wire fence on the bottom
paddock. I am extremly sorry to hear that you
are terrified of pigs.

Yours extremely sincerely

Adele Gardner

Sam van der Velde
Old Tai Tapu Road
RD2
Tai Tapu

Mr Naomi Lopdell
97 Norman's Road
Papanui
Christchurch

November

Dear Mrs Lopdell

I apologise for your skirt and your grazed
elbow. I definitely didn't do it
because I was with Jake watching Robert
calling Julie Johnson. (HE WAS PRETTY GOOD) Lolly has
some excellent photos of you and Daniel running
across the ~~to~~ bottom paddock. You can
PTO »

Ms Love says it may take some time but she will work out
who released Daniel from his cage. She has grave ~~suspi~~
suspicions, she says.
Meanwhile she will seize the opportunity to teach us about
letters of apology...

My teacher is a lovesome creature.

Kate de Goldi

I spent my childhood living and breathing stories. When I wasn't reading, I was writing plays for my sisters, my 42 cousins and my classmates and organising performances. Peter Pan and Wendy lived — I believed — in a gnarled tree at our gate, and Owl from Winnie the Pooh lived in a cherry blossom. I spent many hours plotting and planning with these characters and writing new scenes for them to live and play in. I still live with my own story characters in just the same way.

Kate is an author of three novels for young adults. She is a regular reviewer of children's books on National Radio and teaches writing workshops throughout New Zealand.

Jacqui Colley

I grew up in Africa, climbing trees, swimming in the sea and making huts in the vines, and now I live in New Zealand in a house with a higgledy-piggledy garden by the sea. My garden is like a jungle. An eel lives in the darkest part of the stream and lots of native birds chatter away to me when I am in my studio. Working on picture books is like leaping back to my childhood and a chance for my fantasies and memories to collide.

Jacqui is a painter who exhibits regularly and has work in private collections internationally. She is also a director of a graphic design and new media company.